CLEVER KATE

CLEVER KATE

ADAPTED FROM A STORY BY THE BROTHERS GRIMM

by ELIZABETH SHUB
pictures by ANITA LOBEL

Aladdin Books
Macmillan Publishing Company
New York

Collier Macmillan Publishers
London

Ready-to-Read

10 9 8 7 6 5 4 3 2 1

The art was prepared as black pen-and-ink drawings with overlays done in wash
for blue and yellow. The typeface is Century Expanded, with display set in
Sapphire.

Library of Congress Cataloging-in-Publication Data   Shub, Elizabeth.
Clever Kate.   Summary: Because of her naïveté Kate both loses her hus-
band's treasure and gains it back again.   [1. Folklore—Germany]   I.
Lobel, Anita, ill.   II. Title.   [PZ8.1.S5594C1 1986]   398.2'2'0943
[E]
86-10836   ISBN 0-689-71077-1 (pbk.)

FOR SUSAN C. HIRSCHMAN

One morning Frederick said to Kate,
"I'm going to do some plowing.
   I'll be back in time for lunch."
"I'll have a nice lunch ready," said Kate.
   Frederick and Kate had been
   married a week.

Kate put the house in order.
Then it was time to make lunch.
"I'll make a good tasty sausage
for Frederick," she decided.
And she put a sausage in a pan.
Soon the sausage began to sizzle.

"Some cold beer would go well
with this sausage,"
she said to herself.
Kate took a pitcher
and went to the cellar.

She turned the tap of the barrel
and watched the beer run
into the pitcher.
"How nicely it flows," she thought.
Suddenly she put the pitcher down.

She had just remembered the dog.

She ran up the stairs.

There was the dog

going out the door.

He had the sausage in his mouth.

Kate called him

but the dog raced across the fields.

Kate ran after him.

Soon she was out of breath
and had to stop.
"Well," she said.
"What's gone is gone."
She shrugged her shoulders
and went home.

In the cellar the beer

had run out of the barrel.

It had filled the pitcher and spilled over.

There was not a dry spot on the floor.

Kate had forgotten to turn off the tap.

"Oh my," she said

when she saw what had happened.

"What will Frederick say?"

The sausage was gone.

The beer barrel was empty.

There was a flood in the cellar.

What should she do?

Kate thought and thought.

In the attic was a sack of flour.

Kate hurried to the attic.

She dragged the sack of flour

to the cellar.

The sack hit the pitcher of beer.

The pitcher fell over

and the beer spilled out.

"Oh my," she cried.

"Now there is no beer left

for Frederick to drink.

What shall I do?"

Then she thought, "What's gone is gone."
She untied the sack and
poured the flour over the cellar floor.
"How clean and fresh it looks,"
Kate said.

And she went upstairs

to wait for Frederick.

When she saw him coming,

she ran to meet him.

"Oh, Frederick," she said.

"So much has happened.

I went to the cellar
to get you some beer.
The sausage was frying
and the dog stole it.
I ran after him,
but he ran too fast.
When I came back,
there was no beer left in the barrel.
It was all on the floor.
But do not worry.
I covered it with flour.
The cellar is quite dry now
and everything is fresh and clean."

"Oh, Kate," said Frederick.

"Wasn't it enough to let the dog get
the sausage and let the beer run out?
Why did you have to spoil
our good flour as well?
You should not have done that."

"But, Frederick," said Kate,

"I did not know.

You should have told me."

Frederick thought to himself,
"With such a wife, I will have to be
more careful in the future.
The first thing I must do is
hide the gold coins I have saved."
He asked Kate to bring him a box.

Then he said, "I am going to hide
these yellow buttons in this box.
I am going to bury the box behind
the cow's stall. Kate, promise me
that you will not go near it."

"I promise, Frederick," said Kate.

The next day some peddlers

came to the house.

They had clay pots for sale.

Kate wanted to buy some.

Frederick was not home.

"I have no money," Kate said.

"But my husband has buried a box

filled with yellow buttons

behind the cow's stall.

You may have the buttons

if I may have some pots."

"We must see them first," said the peddlers.

"Very well," said Kate. "But you must

dig up the box yourselves.

I promised Frederick

I would not go near it."

The peddlers went to the barn
and dug up the box.
And when they saw the buttons were
gold coins, they took them and ran off
without even stopping to take their pots.

Kate was very happy.

"Such pretty pots!" she said.

She knocked a hole in each pot

and hung them all around

the kitchen walls.

"What are these?" said Frederick
   when he came home.
"I traded all these pretty pots
   for the yellow buttons in the box
   you buried behind the cow's stall,"
   Kate answered.

And, Frederick, I did just as you said.

I did not go near the barn.

I told the peddlers

to dig up the box themselves."

"Oh, Kate," said Frederick.
"The buttons were gold coins.
   You should not have done that."
"But, Frederick, I did not know
   that they were coins.
   You should have told me."

Kate was very unhappy.

"Let us go after the thieves
    and get our money back," she said.

"That is a good idea," Frederick said.

"Pack up some bread and cheese
    to eat along the way."

Kate got the food ready
and they started out.
Frederick walked very quickly.
At first Kate tried
to keep up with him.

But when she found she couldn't,
she let herself lag behind.
"This is better for me," she thought.
"On the way home
I will be the one ahead."

Soon she came to a hill.

She had almost reached the top

when a cheese fell out of her sack.

It rolled back down the hill.

"I have climbed this hill once," Kate

thought, "and I will not do it again.

Another cheese can run

and bring the first cheese back."

She took a second cheese out

and sent it rolling after the first.

But the second cheese did not bring

the first one back.

"It has lost its way," Kate said.

"I'll send a third to look for it."

And she rolled a third cheese

after the others.

When the three cheeses did not return,

Kate got so angry

she threw a fourth cheese down the hill.

It was her last one.

Kate waited and waited.

But there was no sign of the cheeses.
Finally she called out,
"I will wait no longer!
You may run after me,"
and she walked on.

At last Kate caught up with Frederick.

He had stopped to wait for her

and he was hungry.

"Let us eat," Frederick said.

Kate gave him some bread.

"Where is the cheese?" Frederick asked.

"Oh," said Kate. "They'll be along soon.

One ran away. I sent the others after it."

"Kate," said Frederick.

"You should not have done that."

"Oh dear!" said Kate.

"You should have told me."

As they ate their bread, Frederick said,
"By the way, Kate, did you lock
  the door when you left?"
"Why no, Frederick," said Kate.
"You should have told me."

"Well then," said Frederick,
"go home and make sure it is safe.
And bring back something to eat.
I will wait for you here."
Kate walked back to the house.

She filled a bag with small pears
and a jug with cider.
She locked the upper half of the door
but she took the lower half off its hinges.
"Surely the door will be safer
if I take it with me," she said.
"I can carry it on my back."
She put the door on her back
and started off again.
"If I walk slowly, Frederick will have
a good long rest," she said to herself.
At last she came to the place
where Frederick was waiting.
"I have brought the door, Frederick,"
she said, "to make sure it is safe."

"Oh what a clever wife I have,"
said Frederick.
"Now anyone at all can enter the house.
Well, it is too late to go back now.
Since you have brought the door, Kate,
you must carry it."

"I will carry the door, Frederick,"
  Kate said.
"But the pears and the jug of cider
  are too heavy.
  I will hang them on the door.
  It will carry them."

Frederick and Kate walked on.

Finally they came to a forest.

It was getting dark. They climbed a tree
to be safe from wild animals.

It was not long before three men came along.

They sat down under the tree.

They built a fire and took some
gold coins out of their pockets.

"Look, Frederick," said Kate.

"Here they are.

These are the peddlers.

And those are our gold coins."

Frederick slid down the tree.

The peddlers had their backs to him.

He quickly gathered some stones

and climbed up again.

Then he threw the stones down.

But the stones missed the peddlers.

"The wind is blowing pine cones
off the trees," said one of the peddlers.

Kate was still carrying the door.

"Frederick," she whispered.

"The door is too heavy.

   I must let the pears fall

   to make it lighter."

"No, Kate, not now,"

   Frederick whispered back.

"If you do that,

   the thieves will know we are here."

"I must," Kate said.

"They are too heavy."

   And she emptied the bag of pears.

"Bird droppings,"

   said the second peddler.

The door was still too heavy.

"I must pour out the cider,"
Kate said.

"No, Kate. If you do that,
the peddlers will discover us."

"But I must," Kate said.

And she poured out the cider.

"The dew is falling.

It's almost morning,"

the third peddler said.

"The door is no lighter,"

    Kate said to Frederick.

"May I let it fall now?"

"No! Not now, Kate. You must wait,

    or the peddlers will find us."

"I cannot wait," said Kate.

"I am letting it fall."

    The door came down with a loud crash.

"The devil is coming,"

    the peddlers screamed.

They ran for their lives
and left everything where it lay.
As soon as it grew light,
Frederick and Kate climbed down.
They gathered up the gold coins
and not a single one was missing.

They started for home
and carried the door between them.
"I'm hungry," Frederick said.

"We will eat soon," Kate replied.

"Our cheeses are surely

waiting for us along the way."

And so they were.